Candle's Story

Jez Alborough

LONDON • VICTOR GOLLANCZ LTD • 1988

There was great excitement down in the kitchen at Featherby House, for tonight was the night of the dinner party.

Ruby the maid had spent the whole of that autumn afternoon shining up the silverware to look its very best. It was when she brought the silver candlestick down from the dining room for a polish that she noticed the old candle in it was almost used up; so she replaced it with a brand new candle from a box in the cupboard.

The new candle had never been out of the box before, so to his little eyes the kitchen seemed very bright indeed. Blinking and winking, he wondered what it was that made everything so bright, until he saw Ruby strike a match to light an unlit gaslight.

"Aha," he thought, "so that's where all the light comes from."

Squinting round the table he saw many strange objects: knives, forks, spoons and serving dishes, but among them all he noticed something which looked vaguely familiar.

Like himself it was made of wax and sported on its head a single hair. However, *its* wax body was a wrinkled lump; and the hair, instead of being pure white like his own, was black.

"My goodness," thought the candle, "I'm glad I didn't come out of the box looking like that."

Ruby picked up the candlestick, complete with the new candle, and stepped upstairs to the dining room where she placed it carefully in the centre of the dining room table.

In his new surroundings the candle noticed a strange rhythmic clicking. Looking about the room to see where it was coming from, he saw long velvet curtains by the window, polished mahogany chairs around the table and, to his surprise, in the hallway mirror outside the dining room door he saw himself.

"Gracious," he exclaimed, admiring the clear complexion and the smooth slim body in the mirror's reflection. "Is that me?"

Suddenly he felt rather proud to be standing in the centre of such an elegant room. However, one thing still puzzled him: what *was* that curious noise?

Turning towards the mantelpiece the candle finally discovered the source of the sound.

"What an extraordinary object," he thought, staring at the mantel clock. "All those numbers round his face! And why does he make that silly noise?"

Just then the mantel clock's long hand clicked to number twelve.

Tick tock
       whirr
              dong
                   dong
                        dong
                              . . . he struck his bell
eight times.

In rushed Ruby carrying a large tray. She was late setting the table for the dinner party. At each place she laid glass, napkin and the beautifully polished cutlery. At last everything was ready. Everything, that is, except the candle. He was surprised to see the maid draw a box of matches from her apron pocket.

She struck a match against the side of the box.

"How odd," thought the candle, looking around the room. "What's that for? The gaslights are already lit."

The doorbell rang in the hallway.

"Ruby," called Mr Featherby, "our guests have arrived!"

Ruby hastily leaned over the table with the lighted match.

"Goodness gracious," gasped the candle, "she's coming over here with it."

"Is everything ready, Ruby?" called Mr Featherby as the doorbell rang once more.

"Ready, Mr Featherby," cried Ruby as she lit the candle's wick and scuttled off to receive the guests, shutting the door behind her.

"How very puzzling," mused the candle, looking left and right. "Where *did* that flame go?"

At that moment Mr and Mrs Featherby entered with the guests, and Ruby ushered them to their places at the softly lit table. Once they had settled, she curtsied politely, then served the steaming spinach soup.

The guests supped and chatted, their eyes alive and sparkling with the reflection of the flame which glowed, unbeknown to the candle, above his head.

Mr Featherby nodded to Ruby, who promptly whisked away the soup dishes and returned with an enormous turkey which glistened succulently in the light. Knives and forks shone as they clinked and cut on the china plates.

The guests chortled and chewed, their faces aglow with flickering reds and yellows, but the candle wasn't enjoying himself in the least. He was too busy trying to work out why the top of his head felt so warm.

Mrs Featherby winked to Ruby, who carried off the empty plates and returned with a huge fruit jelly, wobbling in a dish. Clink, tink went the spoons amid sighs of satisfaction, until the very last spoonful had been happily swallowed.

Presently the guests retired full and merry to the drawing room. In bustled Ruby to clear the table; but the candle didn't notice, for he was preoccupied with a peculiar sinking sensation.

Looking down to the table beneath him, he was alarmed to find the surface considerably closer to him than it had been at the beginning of the meal.

Ruby turned off all the gaslights and carried the tray down to the kitchen, without realising for a moment that she had forgotten to do one very last thing . . .

blow out the candle.

"What's happening to me?" cried the candle. "My back is bending and my face feels all droopy."

He looked down at the table and the awful truth dawned on him.

"Help," he shrieked. "I'm shrinking!" He watched in fear as tall black shadows lurched up the walls.

Drip by waxy drip, the table came closer and closer.

Tick tock, tick tock, muttered the mantel clock, as the guests went home and the Featherbys retired for the night.

Drip drop, drip drop, dribbled the wax as Ruby crept upstairs to bed.

Tick tock
    tick tock
        drip drop
            drip drop.

The candle felt hopeless and alone.

Just then he caught sight of something through the open door. It was blue in the centre, with yellow all around; but it was red too, and purple and violet. In fact the more he looked, the more colours he could see. Rising, sinking, they performed a joyful dance. The candle was spellbound by such beauty.

Suddenly he realised what he was looking at: it was his own reflection in the hallway mirror.

"Is that me?" he gasped, understanding at last the true whereabouts of the flame.

"Am I really doing that?" he asked in amazement. Looking above himself he saw that indeed he was. Around the room he watched his colours dancing — along the mantelpiece, over the velvet curtains, and on the smiling face of the mantel clock.

"I must have been doing this all along," cried the candle, "but I was so busy feeling sorry for myself that I didn't see. I brought my own special light to the party; it made my body short and I feel spent, but now I feel so happy that I just don't care."

He remembered the old candle he had seen in the kitchen, and understood.

Feeling at peace, he smiled

closed his eyes

and waited for the dawn.